ISBN 0-86163-489-6

Copyright © 1991 Award Publications Limited

First Published 1991

Award Publications Limited,
Spring House, Spring Place,
Kentish Town, London NW5 3BH

Printed in Belgium

DICK
WHITTINGTON

Illustrated by
RENE CLOKE

AWARD PUBLICATIONS

There was once a little boy named Dick Whittington who lived in a small village.

When he was quite young his father and mother died and there was no one to take care of the boy.

The people in the village were very poor and although they were kind to Dick, they were not able to give him any work.

One day he heard some people talking
about a rich city, London, and he was
determined to find his way there and earn
some money.

He collected all his belongings and tied up everything in a big handkerchief.

It was not very heavy for he did not own much and he carried his bundle over his shoulder and started to walk to London.

It was a long, long way and he was very tired by the time he saw the houses and church steeples of the great city in the distance.

Dick did not find it easy to get work but at last he found a big house where the cook was ready to take a boy to help her in the kitchen.

"You will have to work hard," she told him, "I won't have any idlers in here."

She looked very bad tempered but Dick said he was willing to work for her.

He was put to work at once to scrub the floor, peel potatoes and wash dishes.

Dick did his best but the cook was always cross with him.

She would beat him with her broomstick or ladle whenever she lost her temper.

Poor Dick could not get a good night's sleep for he was put in a garret where the floor and walls were full of holes.

From these the rats and mice came out at night and scampered all over the room.

Dick was in despair until one day when he met a little girl carrying a cat.

She told Dick that her mother had more cats than she wanted and would be glad to give Puss to a good home.

"I will look after her well," said Dick, "and share my dinner with her."

Dick took the cat from her and that night Puss killed many of the rats and mice in the garret. Before long, Dick was able to sleep comfortably.

He became very fond of his pet and always gave her a good platter of food from his own meal as well as a saucerful of milk.

The owner of the big house where Dick
worked had a ship ready to sail to trade
with foreign countries and everyone in the
house was allowed to send something to sell
on the voyage.

Dick had only his cat and he did not want to part with her but he was told that she would be useful on board ship to kill the rats and mice.

"We may sell her abroad for a good price," said the captain.

After the ship sailed, Dick became very unhappy again.

The rats and mice came back to his garret and the cook made fun of him for parting with his cat.

The master and mistress of the house
were kind to Dick and often spoke to him
at his work.

Their little daughter, Alice, was very fond
of him but he decided he must run away.

He packed up his bundle and started to
walk out of London.

He did not know where to go, and
sitting on a milestone looking down on the
city, he heard the bells of Bow Church in
the distance; they seemed to say –

"Turn again, Whittington,
Three times Mayor of London."

"That would be wonderful!" thought
Dick, and feeling more cheerful, he picked
up his bundle and tramped back to London.

Now, the ship with Dick's cat on board had arrived at a foreign port.

Puss had been able to rid the ship of the rats and mice, and had become a great favourite.

The good things from the ship were taken ashore and sold for large sums of money to the people there.

The captain of the ship was asked to dine with the king of the country and found a fine feast prepared at the palace.

But just as
they sat
down –

– a swarm of rats ran across the room and
began eating the food.

"We cannot get rid of them," sighed the
king in despair.

"Have you no cats?" asked the captain.
But no one had heard of such an animal.

The captain hurried
to his ship and
returned with Dick's
cat who very soon
killed every rat and
mouse in the palace.

The king was ready to
pay a huge sum for the cat
and the captain returned to
his ship well pleased with
the money he had earned
for Dick.

After such a successful voyage the ship arrived home full of treasures and money for the merchant and his household.

Everyone gathered around to greet the captain.

"But where is Dick?" asked the captain. "The biggest treasure is for him!"

So Dick was
brought from
the kitchen
and told of
his good
fortune.

"This is wonderful!"
cried the boy. "Now
perhaps I shall one
day become Mayor of
London!"

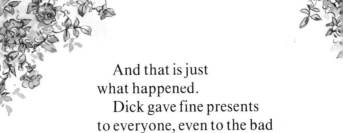

And that is just
what happened.

Dick gave fine presents
to everyone, even to the bad
tempered cook.

He grew up to be a clever and
important man in the City of
London.

He married the merchant's daughter, Alice and was three times Mayor of London.